EMiLY MOUSE'S
Birthday Party

EMiLY MOUSE'S
Birthday Party

Vivian French

Illustrated by Mark Marshall

Orion
Children's Books

ORION CHILDREN'S BOOKS

First published in Great Britain in 2016 by Hodder and Stoughton

1 3 5 7 9 10 8 6 4 2

Text copyright Vivian French, 2016
Illustrations copyright Mark Marshall, 2016

The moral rights of the author and illustrator have been asserted.

A CIP catalogue record for this book
is available from the British Library.

ISBN 978 1 4440 1614 7

Printed and bound in China

The paper and board used in this book are from well-managed forests
and other responsible sources.

Orion Children's Books
An imprint of
Hachette Children's Group
Part of Hodder and Stoughton
Carmelite House
50 Victoria Embankment
London EC4Y 0DZ

An Hachette UK Company
www.hachette.co.uk

www.hachettechildrens.co.uk

For Isabella Poppy,
with much love from Viv xxx

For my god-daughter Molly,
with love, Mark

It was Emily Mouse's birthday.

"I think I'll have a party," Emily
said. "Who shall I ask?"

She made a list.

My friend Fred

My friend Sue

Mary Jean,

Little Jim

"I'll send them a letter." Emily looked at her list. "I hope they can come.

I know! My friend Fred is fond of red, and my friend Sue wears lots of blue. I'll tell them we're going to have red and blue balloons!"

Emily wrote two letters.

Dear Fred,

Please come to my party. There will be red balloons, and a big cake.

Love

Emily

Dear Sue,

Please come to

my party. There

will be blue

halloons, and a

big cake.

Love

Emily

"But what about Mary Jean?"
Emily Mouse rubbed her nose.
"I know!

Mary Jean loves wearing green.

Little Jim's a funny fellow.
What about him?
   Hmmm . . . maybe yellow!"

Emily wrote two more letters.

Dear Mary Jean,

Please come to my party. There will be green balloons, and a big cake.

Love
Emily

Dear Little Jim,

Please come to

my party. There

will be yellow

balloons, and a

big cake.

Love

♡ Emily

"That's that done," said Emily.
"Now, what do I need for my party?"

She made another list.

Orange Juice

Jelly

Sausages on little sticks

Apples and grapes

Sandwiches

Balloons – red, blue, green
and yellow

Cake

Emily went to fetch her
shopping basket. She picked
up her list, and off she went
to the shops.

She went to the supermarket.

"Orange juice and jelly, please,"
Emily said, and she ticked them
off her list.

She went to the butcher.

"Lots of little sausages, please,"
Emily said. She ticked them off
her list.

She went to the greengrocer.

"Apples and grapes, please,"
Emily said. She ticked them off
her list.

She went to the baker.

"A loaf of bread for sandwiches,
please," Emily said.

"I think that's almost everything," Emily said. She looked in the basket for her list . . .

but it wasn't there!

"Oh no," said Emily.

"What shall I do? I'm sure there was something else."

She put down her basket, and
tried to remember.

"I've been to the supermarket, the butcher, the greengrocer and the baker –" Emily stopped, and smiled.

"I know! Balloons! I need to buy balloons!"

Emily Mouse went to the toy shop.

"Please may I have a red, blue, green and yellow balloon?

Red for Fred.

Blue for Sue.

Green for
Mary Jean.

And yellow for
Little Jim. Yellow
is good for him."

Emily put the balloons in her
basket, and she hurried home.

"There!" she said happily.
"Everything's ready for the best
birthday party **ever**!"

She washed her face.

She brushed her whiskers.

She put on her party dress.

Then she sat down to wait . . .

The clock struck four.

"They'll be here any minute,"
she said. "We'll start with the
sandwiches, and finish with cake."

Cake???

"Oh oh oh OH!" squeaked
Emily Mouse. "No no no NO!
I forgot the cake!"

"Nobody will sing Happy Birthday!

I can't blow out my candles!
It won't be the best birthday party
ever! It'll be the **worst**!"

And Emily Mouse began to cry.

"Boo hoo
hoo hoo ..."

Ding dong!

It was the doorbell.

Emily opened the door.

Fred, Sue, Mary Jean and Little
Jim were standing outside.

They were holding
a big box.

"Go away," Emily sobbed.
"It's all gone wrong! I can't have
a party. I forgot to buy a cake!"

"Don't cry, Emily," said Little
Jim. "Look what we made for your
birthday!"

Emily looked in the box . . .

. . . and there was a cake!

The biggest cake she had ever
seen. It had red, blue and green
icing, and the candles were yellow.

"I did the red,"
said Fred.

"And I did the
blue," said Sue.

"I did the green,"
said Mary Jean.

"I chose the
candles," said Little Jim . . .

And Emily Mouse said,
"Do come in!"

And guess what?

Emily Mouse had the **best** birthday party ever!

Can you help
Emily Mouse
mix her colours?

Red and yellow make orange

Blue and yellow make green

Red and blue make purple

What are you going to read next?

Have more adventures with
Horrid Henry,

or save the day with Anthony Ant!

Become a
superhero with Monstar,

float off to
sea with
Algy,

or have your very own Pirates' Picnic.

Grow carrots with

Lottie and Dottie,

make magic with The Witch Dog,

and cast a spell with

The Three Little Magicians.

Enjoy all the Early Readers.